MISSION
CONTAMINATION

The South

Edited By Daisy Job

First published in Great Britain in 2019 by:

Young Writers
Remus House
Coltsfoot Drive
Peterborough
PE2 9BF
Telephone: 01733 890066
Website: www.youngwriters.co.uk

FOREWORD

Young Writers was created in 1991 with the express purpose of promoting and encouraging creative writing. Each competition we create is tailored to the relevant age group, hopefully giving each student the inspiration and incentive to create their own piece of work, whether it's a poem, mini saga or a short story. We truly believe that seeing their work in print gives students a sense of achievement and pride in their work and themselves.

Our Survival Sagas series aimed to challenge both the young writers' creativity and their survival skills! One of the biggest challenges, aside from dodging diseased hordes and avoiding the contagion, was to create a story with a beginning, middle and end in just 100 words!

Inspired by the theme of contamination, whether from a natural mutation, a chemical attack or a man-made experiment gone wrong, their mission was to craft tales of fear and redemption, new beginnings and struggles of survival against the odds. As you will discover, these students rose to the challenge magnificently and we can declare *Mission Contamination* a success.

The mini sagas in this collection are sure to set your pulses racing and leave you wondering with each turn of the page: are these writers born survivors?

CONTENTS

Millie Jane Rahman (11)	49	Theo Chandler	92
Melody Tari (12)	50	Tamsin Meek (11)	93
Emily Powell (11)	51	Bailey Johnson (12)	94
Evelyn Ward (12)	52	Taylor Pritchard (13)	95
Abigail Norman (14)	53	Callum Owen Greenaway (12)	96
Zac Sanders (11)	54	Ryan Brooks (13)	97
Ruth Spring (14)	55	Melody Bragg (12)	98
Alicja Maria Janur (13)	56		
Erin Stokes-Richardson (12)	57		
Kieran Everitt (14)	58		

Rednock School, Dursley

Leona Beech (14)	59	Lewis Elliot Bryant (12)	99
Nicola Maiuga (12)	60	Kayti Miles	100
Rowan Mark Phelps (14)	61	Eowyn Kathleen Barnes-Short (12)	101
Megan Elizabeth Clift (14)	62	Austyn Cole (12)	102
Cameron Beech (12)	63	Halima Wilkins (12)	103
Jonathan Ryan (11)	64	William Johnson (12)	104
Lennon Ben Cooper (13)	65	Isabelle Fowler (12)	105
Sophie Orion (14)	66	Thomas Lightfoot (12)	106
Katie Dando (12)	67	Billy Cadman (12)	107
Hayden Morris (13)	68	Ruby Jean Chandler (11)	108
Sienna Summers (13)	69	Keeva Andersson-Gylden (12)	109
Lucy Phillips (12)	70	Kitty Pain	110
Ruby Harris (12)	71	Miller Exell (11)	111
Imogen Threadingham (13)	72		
Lara Lear (12)	73		

The King's School, Ottery St Mary

Owen Jay Hudson (13)	74	Emiko L'Estrange (13)	112
Thalia Price (13)	75	Daisy Copping (16)	113
Ellie Rice (12)	76	Oliver Matthews (16)	114
Kieran Reed Gowing (12)	77	Scarlett Spencer	115
Chloe Merrick (13)	78		
Zoe Barton (14)	79		

UTC Oxfordshire, Harwell

Georgina Knight (12)	80	Daisy Earl	116
Ethan Robinson (12)	81	Sam Gillies	117
Georgia Heaton (11)	82	Sophie Bardell (15)	118
Maddie May East (12)	83	Joshua Hughes	119
Edgar Alexander Ayers (13)	84	William Thorne	120
Georgie Moss	85	Alex Morgan (14)	121
Kayla White (13)	86	Finnan James Bunce (15)	122
Elsie Hall (12)	87	Samuel Chandler (15)	123
Connor Ryan (12)	88	George Ashby (15)	124
Noah Palmer (12)	89	Aidan Shields (15)	125
Maddie Hobbs (14)	90		
Tyler Hinchliffe (12)	91		

THE MINI SAGAS

The Skinscape

You flinch, simultaneously, with the earth quaking beneath your feet. A shared coincidental moment of twin horror, as you watch owlishly, eyes trained on the most grotesque, human-skinned, eldritch abomination, undulate over. Terrifyingly, your mother's eyes peek out its nest of stolen limbs. Father's smile twists, dotted like stars across the huge, engulfing maw. Bundles of corkscrew arms crawl across the ground, fingers slushing into the dirt, heaving its fleshy density - your teachers, your friends, complete utter strangers - across the weather-drunk cement, to you, the hive mind only knowing one thing, and that being that: *family sticks together.*

H Allison-Soule (16)

Cirencester College, Cirencester

The Prism

They entered the fallout to research and while, initially, they presumed the radiation destroyed life altogether, they then discovered the truth: mass mutation. Like how light distorts through a prism, DNA distorted inside the fallout: adapting biotic code between species, creating unseen, entirely new organisms. Everything was different, even light. Warped, glimmering and manifesting into a spectrum of oil slick spectres. And to her horror, it was somewhat beautiful. Indeed, it caused her to fathom the genetic effect on herself, but, it was only when she saw the squirming beneath her flesh she understood the inescapable danger she was in.

Lauren Taylor (16)
Cirencester College, Cirencester

Sater's Last Stand

Sater ran across the smog hills trying to reach the polystyrene bunker where all the last humans had taken up residence. His mask was an old inheritance which still fought off the smoke. He needed to reach the bunker before sunset or the dreaded gusts of bacteria would severely choke him. Sater lunged across the sharp plastics with ease but was not ready for the next dangerous obstacle - a wide river, consisting of boiling acid stretching ten metres across. He made a raft of thin plastic and got across. Sater had made it. The blistering sunset had started to form.

Andrew Moore (12)
Dawlish College, Dawlish

Blood And Veins

I felt it, a weird sludge, it was horrible having a toxin that infiltrated my skin. Fretfully, I had a bath. Still though it remained inside me. I was apprehensive. I felt solemn. My days, they were numbered. Though I know I'd die, *keep your chin up* is what I thought every second. Even my heart was under pressure. All my life, my grades, my friends, my self-esteem, it had all flown away. Now I was in hospital, it's serious. Tears from crowds of people. It was black and white. *I'm going to die, they'll cut my blood and veins.*

Tito-John Miller (11)
Dawlish College, Dawlish

The Black Death

Caged suffering. Prison of sickness. Temple of pain. Scraping hands. Desperate shrieks. Forced breaths. Rushed prayers. God will save us. Derelict buildings. Soulless homes. Crying children. Sullen elders. Empty eyes. Still hearts. God, save us. Yet we live. Meaningless survival. Futile efforts. God will save us. Rancid spewing. Erupting boils. Wasting skin. Wasted blood. Flies swarming. Rats scurrying. Plague corners. Apostle of pestilence. The gates creak. Doctors enter. Raven men. They watch. They leave. They learn. They condemn. We pray. God will save us. We cough, we choke, we all fall down. God won't save us. God isn't here.

Henry Hutchings (17)
Devonport High School For Boys, Plymouth

It's Happened

It's happened, of course it has. I don't know why I ever doubted it, but this soon? Well, I suppose I'd better stop just sitting here and worrying, I'd better start doing something. Start stopping this, well, this contamination. I had better start now. But how? *How?* My brother is in hospital, all my friends are in hospital, my father is in hospital, even the doctors are in hospital. *How on earth am I meant to do this?*
Wait, Philip, breathe, there we go. Well, I'll start with... I... feel... a... bit... I-I'll be okay, I think. "Mum!"

Harry Pickard (12)
Devonport High School For Boys, Plymouth

New Creation

My fiancée came in sobbing. "What happened?" I pleaded. I couldn't afford to see her cry; not then. She was the reason I bothered getting through each day.

"Father j-just had a massive lab explosion."

That stabbed at me, cut me into pieces. That's when it happened, a magnificent smell drifted into the room; intoxicating me. It was... beautiful. I felt my skin burn; a new creation born. I looked at my eternal love. I despised her, she was in the way of my sole purpose. I lunged at her. Her skin smelled so awfully poisonous...

Alfie Godfree (12)
Devonport High School For Boys, Plymouth

Rescue

One hundred days. I've spent one hundred days sat waiting. But what am I waiting for? I think it's clear that no one will rescue us now, I'm only prolonging the inevitable. I don't even know what I need rescuing from. It didn't seem like a threat, hell, it wasn't even 'it' a few days ago. It wiped out humanity, littering the streets with rotting remains. I have advice though: die and pray for salvation. I have found even the most agnostic of man finds fortune in prayer. If you wish to fight, then good luck. I choose to die.

Rudi Gibbs (13)
Devonport High School For Boys, Plymouth

Status: Infected

"You okay in there?" I said as a growl emitted from the cockpit. Another growl sounded from the cockpit. Me and the crew looked at each other as if someone would suddenly know what to do. Unexpectedly, the captain was stood there giving off a ghostly glow. Oozing sores covered his face and he was snarling. He had the virus. I knew what I had to do. It was either this or a painful death from the virus. I picked up my pistol and shot the pilot. That night everyone saw the blazing helicopter fall into the sea and explode.

Billy Carlton (13)
Devonport High School For Boys, Plymouth

Metamorphosis

My veins were glowing. I heard a constant rhythm to my booming heartbeat. All I had to do was keep fighting. I sweated, vomit oozing from my mouth as I lay in agony. My veins pulsed, my heartbeat slowed, my pupils dilated. I lay there as my flesh pruned up and crimson blood exited my eyes along with a single tear. I had failed, they had got to me. Suddenly, my heart stopped suddenly like the end of a song. My muscles relaxed. I lay still, relaxed, at peace. My time was up. My eyes opened. I craved one thing...

Angus Kerr (13)
Devonport High School For Boys, Plymouth

Feverish

The rash was spreading, pulsing, hurting. Marcello panted breathlessly, perspiration dripping down his neck as he frantically clawed his burning arms. They were covered in crimson and purple blotches which itched agonisingly. "Good Goddess." He screwed his stinging eyes shut, silently praying for the sweet release of death as he lay alone on the scorching sand, body contorting violently. *Is this how I die?* Marcello wondered. The metallic taste of blood filled his mouth. He thought briefly of his younger brother - where was he now? Pain stabbed at Marcello's chest; slowly, his muscles relaxed and he succumbed to his sickness.

Natalie Catherine Ruby (16)
Fernhill School, Farnborough

The End: New Beginning

Land that was once vibrant, is now nothing more than charcoal and ash. Above, a layer of soot hangs like a haze, partially obscuring the fulgent sun. Empty cities stand broken like defeated warriors whilst the streets are inhabited by the shadows of fallen men, bodies scattered like ragdolls. The living dead has wiped out the entire world and nobody has been able to stop them. Alpha radiation leaking from the labs of the Global Physics research and development centre initiated this catastrophe. One man has survived, is it possible that his heart is the last one beating on Earth?

Lauren Adriana Slater (11)
Fernhill School, Farnborough

The Giant Poisonous Cloud Rose Into The Sky

It began. The machines are pumping poisonous fog out quicker than you can imagine. Fog covers the sky like a blanket. I panic, I cannot do anything but watch, watch through this tiny window. I think I'm going crazy. The noise, the noise of everything! The machines, people, footsteps, talking, everything around me. Yet I'm stuck in these chains, slowly cutting deeper into my skin. The fog has covered everything. *Splash!* Acid rain hits the window. I strike at the glass, but all I can do is watch. The door opens. Man stand at the door. "Time to go."

Jasmine Pheasant (14)
Fernhill School, Farnborough

The Rash Was Spreading, Pulsing, Hurting

It was like I was infected by something, it was itchy, painful. My arm was red raw. It was irritating me, I couldn't handle it. It wouldn't stop rushing up my arm. It was massive like a thousand mosquitos sucking blood out of my arm. My heart was racing, beating faster than it would after a sprint race. I couldn't control it. I couldn't breathe. Hyperventilating. I had to do something to stop it. The worst case was chopping my arm off. I didn't think there was a cure. I grabbed the knife. *Slice.* Blood squirted everywhere, screaming and crying.

Levi Mitchel Collins (15)

Fernhill School, Farnborough

The Rash Was Spreading, Pulsing, Hurting

Throbbing, killing like there's no tomorrow.

The rain became heavier; hail crashed down on the vehicles. I had to run. Blistering winds and storms appeared. In the distance, something was beaming!

The rash grew by the second. I needed to be cured. My legs started to tremble. It felt like poison going through my bloodstream. It felt like I was going to suffer and suffer until I next closed my eyes. My legs dropped and fell to the concrete ground. Boiling blood ran down my head. This was the moment, I knew I couldn't figure out what this poison was.

Harvey-Lee Szymczyk (14)
Fernhill School, Farnborough

A Bad Day In The Lab

The last drop falls into the test tube, there's an awkward silence as the mixture reacts. Two metres away from the tube waiting to see what awaits us. *Bang!* A drop of iodine connects with my skin, something feels weird under my skin. 999! An ambulance is called and arrives in a heartbeat. The pain grows until I feel no more. Scan after scan. Finally, they see an issue. There seems to be potassium in the mixture causing deadly reactions with my body. My sight goes fuzzy. My body starts to feel extremely weak. *Beep! Beep! Beep!*

Jack McLean (14)
Fernhill School, Farnborough

The Fog

A young boy is travelling the barren city, seeing a green, slow-moving fog creeping towards him. Terrified, he sprints away from the fog, meeting five people who seem to also be fleeing the area. He overhears them. "We have sent so many in, none have come out alive." He panics.
After a minute he walks over to them and asks, "Where is everyone?"
Petrified, one of the people tell him all of the others have been lost to the fog's grasp.
He pauses then fog is right in front of him... There is no escape!

Brandon Doody (12)

Fernhill School, Farnborough

The Test Tube

The last drop fell into the test tube, mixing with the acid. The solution bubbled and overflowed. The ink-black liquid spilt, spread across the lab table and onto the tile floor. We watched through the glass window, gazed at it with wide eyes, horrified at the sight. The solution grew and spread up the walls like claws and vines. Slowly the white lab was pitch-black, like the deep sea. In the silence, all to be heard was the slime dripping from the ceiling into a pool of what looked like nothing. This is what was living in us.

Wendy Sedlackova (14)
Fernhill School, Farnborough

My Biggest Fear

Something scuttled under my skin, something small but frightening. My heart was beating faster than ever before. My breathing gradually slowed down and I reached for my chair. As I grabbed my chair, my legs suddenly collapsed and my sight became a blur. I began to feel faint and my head was in a whirl. Although it was only an unknown bug, to me it was like it wanted to chew me up until my insides came rushing out. Bugs were my biggest fear, however big or small they were, they still made my heart stop. Then I collapsed.

Isabella Mae Barbrook (12)
Fernhill School, Farnborough

Burrowers

Something scuttled under my skin and into my veins. I watched as the bulge advanced up my arm, past the crevasse of my cubital fossa and burrowed its way through my biceps. My breathing sped up but I made sure not a sound left my lips, it would only attract more. We nicknamed them burrowers for their unique ability to burrow through skin. At first, we didn't know what they were, a disease, a creature, a parasite? All that was known was that people were dying and they were dangerous. We needed to fight back.

Charlie Grantham (13)
Fernhill School, Farnborough

I Have A Bug (Literally)

Something scuttled under my skin, it moved through my body. I instantly felt sick and faint. Everyone in my class stared at the moving bump in my arm as I ran for the door.

I sat in the office and when my mother walked through the door I rushed to her and tried to hug her with my arm in my school bag. She took me to the doctors.

He said I'd be fine. Just get rest. I cried. My mother wasn't happy so we went to the hospital. I had a life-threatening condition.

I have a virus forever.

Brooke Durston (12)
Fernhill School, Farnborough

Risk

I finally emerged from the underground bunker. I peeked out my head slowly. I was stuck in the bunker, nowhere to go. We had no supplies left, so I could not hide from the zombies. I looked everywhere. It was filled with dead bodies, scattered everywhere, all over the place. I stepped out of the bunker. I knew I had to get food and water fast. I could see a small forest in the distance. It was a risky run but I went for it, looking for food and water, hoping the zombies wouldn't kill me!

Rhys Baker (13)
Fernhill School, Farnborough

Desperate Times, Desperate Measures

The man's body arched unnaturally. His mouth twisted into a pained grin. Coated in blood like a clown's smile, hot, purple boils sprouted along his neck and shoulders. Black sludge oozed from his eyes and Doctor Kim stared in horror. The bio suit suddenly grew hot and she backed away. Crawling towards her, what was left of the man snarled and groaned like a beast. Kim took a gun, pointed it to the man's head and fired.

"Subject 266 was unsuccessful, immediate termination required. Bring in 267."

A woman came in this time and Doctor Kim smiled grimly. She began.

Caitlin Jamie Fowler (16)

Honiton Community College, Honiton

The Spores

It started a few years ago; a few spores landed in my garden. We didn't notice them at first but when my cat ate one she started acting really weird - she would keep on scratching us.

We went to see the vet. Rose bit the vet and then started to vomit a cloud of yellow dust that soon disappeared.

The next day was even worse. Rose had a large mushroom on her back that sprayed the same dust as before and my mum had the same mushroom on her head. Outside, even more people had different mushrooms on their heads...

Lochlann Wrigley
Kingsbridge Community College, Kingsbridge

Despair

The test tube sizzled and bubbled. Then after a few seconds, nauseating radiation spread rapidly across the Isles of Scilly. David pulled his special mask down and cried in terror, "Noooooooo! I didn't mean to spread the disease across the world."

Men ran for their families as they saw the green chemical spread from the new lab. Children cried out in horror and women hurried them inside. David looked out and groaned in despair. Will this be the end?

Reuben Miles
Kingsbridge Community College, Kingsbridge

The Contamination Curse

A lazy scientist had thrown some chemicals into a sewer, they reached the water system, contaminating it. People were drinking mysterious chemicals, they were turning into some sort of alien beings roaming the streets, infecting other people. Next, food poisoning happened, the clouds turned green, trees were falling by the second, plants were rotting, air was running out. The human population was going down rapidly. Buildings were falling apart, dust was becoming an issue, weird gas started travelling down streets knocking people out. Stone was becoming super weak and the ground started cracking and falling in. Humans were becoming extinct.

Lucas Mullins (11)
Maidenhill School, Stonehouse

The Radioactive Chemical

Callum the crazy scientist was messing with dangerous experiments. A radioactive wave of chemicals exploded and Callum got mutated. The mutation was contaminating. Slowly, Earth was spreading mutations. People were trying to think of solutions. Aircraft took off Earth, but there was not enough for even a quarter of Earth's population! Fear was all over the atmosphere, you couldn't look anywhere without there being a mutation. Earth's population was under fifty thousand, the human race was almost gone... As the last humans slowly and dreadfully went with terrorized fear. The lands went dull and the sun shone bright and proud.

Tyrese Elisha Adegbamigbe (12)
Maidenhill School, Stonehouse

It All Goes Wrong!

It began three months ago, the man who's killed half the human race. Jonathon Jacobo. His failed genetic mutation promised us high senses, so sharp you'd be able to hear a pin drop in the hay. Now half the human race had been contaminated. One creature has been captured and was being studied on by Doctor Phil. Out of the blue, "Start the transmission device, *now!*" It took half an hour to turn on. Almost immediately all research facilities and underground bunkers received a blueprint for curing the genetically altered dangerous zombie creatures. Was this the beginning of the end?

Mason Cunningham (11)
Maidenhill School, Stonehouse

Experiment 362

'Dear Diary, I have been the galaxy's only scientist for decades. I have created every man that walks on Mars. But, can I make my brothers better? I could create something the universe has never seen before. I shall call it Experiment 362'.

A millennium later... 'Dear Diary, my beloved 362 is an amazing success. I plan to replicate her, but she has emotions? I have never seen this before. I must try a different chemical'.

'Dear Diary, I must destroy all knowledge of 362, she is a dangerous threat'.

'Dear Diary, Experiment 362 got out. May God save us'.

Lucie Meredith (13)

Maidenhill School, Stonehouse

Earth's Last Chance

"No, no, please. I'll give it to you just don't hurt me." The man was now cowering in the corner. *Bang!* The gunshot could be heard all around, bringing lots of the mutants. The man ran into the derelict building to the meeting point previously arranged but as he got there he saw a truly fearful sight, the resistance.

"It's over doctor, give us back the cure."

"Never, the world must become mutated."

So began a standoff which lasted for minutes, becoming tenser by the second, until the mutants stormed the room quickly ending it all...

Liam Emery (14)
Maidenhill School, Stonehouse

The Blindfold

Blindly, Sarah trecked through the jungle unable to see a thing, until she heard a rustle. What could it be? Sarah didn't care. She ran as fast as she could until she ran into a tree, she was out cold.

Ten minutes later, a boy found her and brought her into his tree house and woke her up. "Ahh, what are you doing?" shouted Sarah.

"I'm trying to save you and be quiet."

"Why should I trust you? You just kidnapped me!" exclaimed Sarah.

"Because I'm trying to save you."

Before they knew it, they were killed by the infection.

Joseph Anderson (11)
Maidenhill School, Stonehouse

24 Hours - Dead Or Alive

They touch you, you're dead, you won't survive. You're dead within the next twenty-four hours. You can feel them crawling along your bones, flying around your stomach, no end to the pain. Once you die your soul stays alive, you touch another soul, you're dead. They walk around looking like normal human beings, nothing different except they have no heart. You are alone soon enough. The world will be full, full of lost souls, parents infecting children, children infecting friends. Is this the end or will I fear no more horror? Can I survive this terrible outbreak, yes or no?

Ruby Hatherall (13)
Maidenhill School, Stonehouse

The End Of The World

We finally emerged from the underground bunker, it had been months since the infection started and chaos was still prominent. The flesh-eaters still trudged around brainless. No one knows how the breakout of the infection started, whether it was a DNA mutation or chemicals. We can't ask anyone because they are either dead or have turned. The super breed are blind but seem to be hypersensitive and have super hearing. Their bodies are charred and soaked in blood with rotten teeth and sad eyes like they've realised what they have become. This is what the end of the world looks like.

Ellie Dowden (13)
Maidenhill School, Stonehouse

The Unknown Disease

The giant poisonous cloud rose into the sky. The wave of contamination was unknown. It was spreading across the city. It must stop, it must stop before it wiped out the population. But it seemed as though there was no cure. As more and more people began to discover the anonymous disease, the belief that they would survive decreased. Over time, many people started to severely struggle to handle the disease. It was getting intense. Had everyone been contaminated? Was everyone going to survive? The deadly disease had killed thousands. It was going to kill more! Would it stop?

Eva Casey (14)
Maidenhill School, Stonehouse

Test Subject 7

Test Subject 7 might be the only successful test of thousands tested. He is the only one who didn't react to the virus. The virus makes people's ears bleed and become violent. He seems to be like normal... Through loudspeaker in lab, "The doors are released and the genetically modified beings are escaping..." Ben is an intern but he knew this could be his last living day on the disease-filled planet called Earth. He sprinted to the hall of the underground bunker. He saw a creature standing, looking at him. It ran at him.
Ben's current whereabouts: Unknown.

Will Gamble (13)
Maidenhill School, Stonehouse

Test Subject A

Test Subject A is unaccounted for. Everyone pay attention, don't let him bite you otherwise you will become contagious, contaminated and will have twenty-four hours to live. Don't touch anyone because the disease spreads by touch. My advice to you all is to not touch anything or anyone, including food and drink because that could also have been affected by the disease. If you see someone get bitten then run away really fast. If everyone gets bitten then that will be the end of the human race. Symptoms include: skin turning blue, eyes begin to bulge and teeth getting sharper.

Kalila McLaughlin (13)
Maidenhill School, Stonehouse

Goodbye

Something scuttled under my skin. *This is it*, I thought. It was only a matter of minutes before my brain became overloaded and I was erased from this world. It was like an alarm in my head: "Brain overload in T-minus ten minutes." No one would know at least. At first, I thought it was an itch but I noticed an overlap in my skin and knew it was over. "Brain overload in T-minus five minutes." I grabbed an apple, eating it slowly. "Overload in T-minus one minute."
"Goodbye world," I said to myself. Then the world went blank. Death.

Isaac Lee Harper (14)
Maidenhill School, Stonehouse

Happiness, It's Contagious

It all began with the dolphins, if it was the pollution or the poaching, eventually the dolphins tried to become friends with humans. They tried things like playing with humans and it was this fueled ambition which led to our happy Earth. The dolphins used their knowledge to make nanobots to eradicate sadness. First, it was hated but as soon as grief spread, happiness became central for survival. The nanobots were equipped with teeth to force happiness, which meant that if one person died everyone that grieved them were exterminated. This led to the eradication of the human race.

Peter Scrivens (12)
Maidenhill School, Stonehouse

Summer Fog

The rash spread but what had caused this disease? Fog in summer, this couldn't be right. I stumbled outside to receive the post and the pain shot through my body from head to toe. My heart rate was off the charts, my skin stung. I, Dr Brown, couldn't even explain this occurrence. People all around me screamed with unbelievable pain as their skin disintegrated. I pulled myself inside, but it was too late. Fog in my house, in my room, every nook and cranny. It was airborne. It destroyed everything and everyone. There was no stopping this horrific contamination.

Freya Cook (14)
Maidenhill School, Stonehouse

Zombie Apocalypse

Some careless scientists were doing an experiment when suddenly it exploded, sending gases around the world. But the thing about these gases was that they had the power to turn all humans into zombies. There was a secret underground bunker that the army had built a long time ago, just in case anything like this happened. They were searching for survivors, especially nurses and scientists. The scientists could help to discover the cure to stop a zombie apocalypse. In the bunker, there were a lot of beds and ration boxes for forty-eight hours. There wasn't a lot of time left!

Connor Timbrell (12)
Maidenhill School, Stonehouse

The Infected

The lab door was trembling. The infected were almost in. The cure was almost done, the sweat was dripping down my face. *Smash!* The glass in the door had smashed, the infected's disfigured faces were peeking through. "Almost done," I kept saying to myself. The hinges on the door were shaking and the screws were slowly coming off. *Bang!* The door swung open, the cure was ready. I picked it up and chucked it at the infected. There disfigured bodies started to show the smooth human faces. I had saved a few, but there were many more infected to go...

Tom Gibbs (12)
Maidenhill School, Stonehouse

The Poisonous Snake

Silently walking through the dark forest I heard a rumbling in the sky. I decided to go home. Something rattled between my feet. "What is that?" I questioned myself. "Please someone help me," I screamed. Before I knew it I was on the floor.

Waking up, after a horrible feeling, I lay in hospital, the rash on my ankles was spreading fast. My brown bumpy skin felt horrible. After my terrible tasteless antibiotics, I felt a lot better. However, I had to stay in hospital for another two days. I discovered that a poisonous snake had bitten me...

Sienna Huggins (12)
Maidenhill School, Stonehouse

Knocking On Death's Door

The world is knocking on death's door. People are dropping like flies. There are only five of us left who remain uninfected. I have one mission: to shut down the virus by dropping an immunisation serum into the atmosphere. It is a suicide mission meant for disaster. The killers catch me and find my insides. The pain is spreading, pulsing, hurting my lungs, desperately searching for any escape, helpless. My thoughts fill with panic, my heart racing, thumping. One mission and I failed, failed all of humanity. *Atishoo, atishoo, gasp!* We all fall dead...

Charlotte Hatch (14)
Maidenhill School, Stonehouse

Time's The Key

Right now, millions of people are dying because of one species that is invisible to the naked eye. This tiny creature is sinking into the hearts of many, the death count is increasing rapidly and isn't going to stop. But nobody fear, Super Simon is here with this new cure. He calls it the 'Heart Spray'. This amazing substance rebuilds hearts in three seconds. However, if Simon doesn't reach everyone in time there is no way he can finish this task but Simon's up for the challenge. Simon is now across the ocean when he drops the spray. Oh dear!

Oakley James (12)
Maidenhill School, Stonehouse

Time Contamination

"I have been sent on a mission to travel back in time and observe the battle of Waterloo," spoke James the time traveller. He bounded into his time machine. *Whoosh!* He was gone. Suddenly, he heard a bang. He swung the door open. He saw two smartly dressed soldiers with their mouths open in awe. One yelped, "You have just killed Lord Wellington." I think it was time for him to leave. When he returned to the present, he found that everyone was speaking French. It couldn't be! The English must have lost the battle all because of me.

Edward Eric Percival (11)
Maidenhill School, Stonehouse

Bad Eggs

An explosion at the Nuclear Power Plant caused a piece of new plutonium to fly into the drinking water at a nearby farm. As chickens drank the water, any eggs laid were infected causing people who ate them to fall ill with bad headaches and insomnia. We thought it would be contained within the host's body and die out as people discovered the eggs were to blame, however, the viral infection evolved to ensure its survival, resulting in being able to spread to other hosts through touch. The infection has taken over, only a few survivors remain. Send help!

Jonty Brown (13)
Maidenhill School, Stonehouse

This Is It

This is it, we're running out of time and supplies. There's only four of us left. The bitten virus has wiped out everyone else. We think. Others have looked for what we need, food, water, cure? They could still be out there, searching. We're preparing for tomorrow in an attempt to see what's out there, what we're dealing with. If it's safe. But for now, we rest...

Today we leave, we're ready. I open the doors, darkness. I haven't seen the outside world in months. I want to take it all in but I have a mission. This is it...

Maya-Rosa Blackie (13)
Maidenhill School, Stonehouse

The Cloud

The giant poisonous cloud rose into the sky. People fell to the ground in front of me gasping for air, holding their chests. Their bodies disappeared into the air. What happened to all those innocent people, they just disappeared into thin air, swallowed up by the thick cloud? People screamed unbearably trying to hold on to their life. This cloud was thick, green and toxic and was all around this city, there was no escape. People were getting swallowed up, their bodies were disintegrating immediately into little pieces. Will this be the end of the human race?

Lucia Hinchliffe (13)
Maidenhill School, Stonehouse

The Bite

The night was calm, a full moon was beaming, people were falling to the ground. Their skins looking like snow. Teeth falling out, fangs growing and the need for blood. *How long is it going to be before the whole world is affected?* thought Callum. What was happening was a terrible thing. He ran out onto the streets, desperate for a place to hide. He heard footsteps behind him as he sprinted down the road, the footsteps were getting closer. *Crunch!* A bite on the neck. He was out cold. His pulse stopped. Callum was dead, his soul wasn't...

Millie Jane Rahman (11)
Maidenhill School, Stonehouse

Space Syndrome

It's the year 2052, thirty years since the deadly disease killed everyone on this planet except me... or so I thought. The disease originally started in Kennedy Space Centre when astronaut Nicky came back from Saturn and reported her findings. However, she didn't know she had the most deadly disease ever created. By the time they found out it was airborne it was too late. It had spread worldwide and everyone was gone. I felt lost, lonely and terrified. That was in 2022, however, I thought I was the only one left until I realised I wasn't alone...

Melody Tari (12)
Maidenhill School, Stonehouse

The Apocalypse

The infection had spread, it had infected these creatures, these monsters. They had long slimy hands, they were extremely thin and their heads shaped like eggs. As I watched other people running for their lives with bats, knives and other weapons to destroy the creatures, I felt something touch my shoulder. I screamed, "Argh!" I sighed in relief as I felt Dr Bob touch my shoulder. We were nearly at the lab. I ran inside and put the antidote in the machine. I felt something touch my shoulder. I screamed but nobody heard me scream. Would I survive?

Emily Powell (11)
Maidenhill School, Stonehouse

Shrivelled Away...

An injection, what's happening? Nearly everyone has died! They're lying by my feet! As I make eye contact with someone they shrivel to my feet! Everyone's bodies shrivel and they slowly and painfully fall to the ground, however, every time someone falls to my feet something scuttles under my skin and it feels like power and pain mixed together! My family and friends are dead so there's nobody I can ask for help! I feel anxious, angry and sad! What is this feeling? Will the human race end? Will I have to sacrifice my life or is there a cure?

Evelyn Ward (12)
Maidenhill School, Stonehouse

12 Hours - Life Or Death

The rash spread and burned through his body, in less than twelve hours he was dead. It all started on the morning of nineteenth September 1964. As he climbed out of the bed he scratched his wrist. At this point, he knew he was doomed. All over the newspapers were stories about people dying from a scratch that formed to a rash, that spread around the body, in twelve hours they were dead. As the pain reached his heart, he curled up, praying that the rash would spread quicker, killing him quicker, so this pain would disappear. "Please kill me now!"

Abigail Norman (14)
Maidenhill School, Stonehouse

Doomsday

It all happened in an instant. It was mass disruption, then the fumes of the chemicals were released. This happened two days ago, during detention. Only three of us remained, Jake, Joe and I. We emerged from the house. Glowing green mutations slouching stood there. They saw us? We hurried as quick as possible. Joe tripped, survival of the fittest, we had to leave him... "Sprint!" I bellowed, the mutants were faster than us. We hid. We heard crackling and barking. We split and my flashlight died. I heard a snap, silence then a deafening scream...

Zac Sanders (11)
Maidenhill School, Stonehouse

Mosquito Mystery

Last week the world was upside down. People were insane, running in the streets like zombies. It was like a monster had taken over the human race. There was a contagious rash going around, caused by mosquitos that were poisoned. The rash was spreading, hurting and killing the whole population - red, spotty rashes over the body. It was a disaster. A box was found by a clever scientist and inside was the cure. He scattered it everywhere and suddenly it was like it never happened, it went back to normal and no one was dead. It's still a big mystery...

Ruth Spring (14)
Maidenhill School, Stonehouse

Experiment 13

"They are trapped," says Professor Two. He slowly walks to them, while them being trapped, and taps them on their head. "Everything will be okay, don't worry." Professor Two goes out of the glass room and pulls the lever. A lot of chemicals are poured on to the poor sad people.

"Experiment thirteen is successful," says Professor One with a sad tearful look. The people slowly turn into dust which forms a triangle on the ground.

"Why did we do this?"

"Because we had a job to finish."

Alicja Maria Janur (13)
Maidenhill School, Stonehouse

Escape Route

After weeks of waiting in a toxic, claustrophobic underground bunker, me and Jessica were trying to find a way to escape. Hour after hour, time passed by. The sulphuric smells got stronger. We tried everything and eventually found a way out. We had to do it before the zombies came back.
We climbed through the broken glass and ran into a dark forest. The silence was deafening. As rain began to fall, we smelt a certain smell. Sulpher. Once again, we were running. We hid under trees. My tree moved. My tree talked. It was dragging me... I was dead.

Erin Stokes-Richardson (12)

Maidenhill School, Stonehouse

Day Z

The cure had to be somewhere. All we needed was an answer to all the questions we had. How? Why? When? And the big one... was there a cure? I'm writing a diary so if someone finds me they know how I survived. I need food, water. I'm about one mile away from the supermarket. It will be dangerous. There's too many of them. We don't call them anything because we don't know what they are. They kill, they're deadly. They're fast. They're everywhere. I'm in New York. Only a couple of people live. Will I make it or die?

Kieran Everitt (14)
Maidenhill School, Stonehouse

Touch

Touch - something I longed for. I would have given everything to be left isolated but now what I wouldn't give to have company. Humanity was over. Nobody else was alive and I was left to find the cure, I paced around an abandoned lab. Surely the cure had to be there. I tiptoed, searching every snippet of space. I had never been so conscious of my senses: scared, worried, discouraged. I realised I couldn't fix someone else's naive mistakes. I lay down by the table and scrunched my knees tightly to my head. The end wasn't my desire...

Leona Beech (14)

Maidenhill School, Stonehouse

Transparent Acid

Mischievously, human Satan was thinking of a cunning plan to seek revenge on those nasty humans. Aha! He knew what to do. Quietly, he crept into the human's baths, poured a transparent acid into them and now he was thinking that when they climbed in their skin would start to rot away. Mwhahaha! The disease was spreading, pulsing, horror rose and soon everyone was forced to stay indoors, not to take any showers or baths until they solved the problem. Everyone was very scared. What would happen to the food if it ran out? Who would save us? Argh!

Nicola Maiuga (12)
Maidenhill School, Stonehouse

The Fateful Rash

The rash was spreading, pulsing, hurting. This was the last thing I remember before passing out. When I awoke everything seemed off, though everything looked the same the atmosphere was weird. What once used to be the busy streets of London was now deserted, piles of litter were everywhere. I sat up and looked around, I heard moaning from what seemed like miles away, the moaning came closer, it was right behind me. I turned around and there was a man there, his skin melting off. The only instinct I had was to run. Earth would never be the same...

Rowan Mark Phelps (14)
Maidenhill School, Stonehouse

Don't Drink, You'll Die

All the water has been contaminated but still, people drink it. Whilst people are dying from drinking it no one knows what's actually been in the water to make it contaminated but it's deadly. We need to find a solution soon otherwise every single human being will be wiped from this earth. All my family are dead. It's just me left. They've been trying to find a solution for weeks but they can't. At this rate, everyone will be gone and that means it will be the end of the human race forever. This is not going to be solved...

Megan Elizabeth Clift (14)
Maidenhill School, Stonehouse

Beware Of Subject A!

Where is everyone? Why aren't they here? Why isn't anybody picking up the phone? These were all of the questions running through my head at this moment in time. Suddenly a piece of paper caught my eye, I ran over to it, hoping it would be the answer to all of my questions. I looked at it, but all it said was 'Beware of Subject A!' This left more questions in my head: *who is subject A? Who wrote this note? Did a mysterious creature named Subject A take or do something to my family? Crunch*, I turned...

Cameron Beech (12)
Maidenhill School, Stonehouse

The Impossible Task

The rash was spreading, pulsing, hurting. My skin was disintegrating. I didn't know what to do. It was impossible to save everyone, either we would die of dehydration or disintegration. I needed to find a cure, but time was running out. How was this a possible task without the right equipment? The bunker, it must be there.

I ran to the bunker, opened the large metal doors and made a run for the antidote. Since the people were still alive they could still drink it, but sadly it was too late, my other arm had rotted away; it was over.

Jonathan Ryan (11)
Maidenhill School, Stonehouse

The Attack Of The Demagon

It's the year 2069, 20 years after Dr Smith did human testing with the parasite Demagon, the Demagon was to give humans special powers such as mind control. However, Test Subject #011 escaped and spread the parasite all over the world. Now I was trapped inside my lab and infected humans were breaking down my titanium door. I ran over to my locker and grabbed a gun. I aimed at the door and waited. Suddenly the door slammed to the floor, infected humans came swarming in. They turned themselves and gazed at me. I closed my eyes and fired...

Lennon Ben Cooper (13)
Maidenhill School, Stonehouse

Deadly Virus

My name's Bessa. I worked in a research lab for the Umbrella Corporation which was underground. We all had a room with two single beds, a desk and a lamp. I shared a room with my friend Molly. I always knew my job was dangerous and risked lots of lives, not only mine. Last week seven scientists were introduced to a bird virus, however, it wasn't like anything I had worked on before. This one was type B, an extremely deadly virus that was contagious. We didn't know this. After just one hour of contact, it caused seven deaths...

Sophie Orion (14)
Maidenhill School, Stonehouse

The Bite

Something scuttled under my hand, I felt small teeth sink into my finger. The teeth marks were made by a mosquito. The bite turned into a lump, the lump became green, slowly spreading up my arm. I felt numb like my brain had gone, no thoughts remained. Everything went black, screams surrounded me. My eyes opened, my feet were leading the way. My green ugly feet led me to my neighbours, shop owners, my boss and fellow workers. I devoured their brains and the same green colour was growing on them. I did not know what had happened that day.

Katie Dando (12)
Maidenhill School, Stonehouse

The Fight Closet

Charlie hid in the closet. They were breaking down the door. "Help!" she screamed but nobody could hear her. The beast entered the room. It had sharp, blood-coloured teeth and claws and green bony bubbles all over its head. Charlie hid in the closet. The beast ran to the closet and cut her leg. Blood was oozing out as she silently screamed. She tried to kick the beast away and tried to close the door of the closet. More beasts came and pulled the door off. They lifted her up and put her in their crimson teeth. Charlie was dead.

Hayden Morris (13)
Maidenhill School, Stonehouse

Aftermath

The giant poisonous cloud rose into the sky, creating layers of darkness across the lifeless land. The air was a gloomy green blanket with a toxic smell. Everyone was dead. I stumbled out behind a jagged rock. My suit was of a strong protective rubber, the layers of glass in front of my eyes kept away the sting, just like the suit. I'm not sure how long my suit would keep out the radiation, everyone had already been infected. I stumbled over something with burns of green over the body. A human which was alive but not a human now...

Sienna Summers (13)
Maidenhill School, Stonehouse

The Scandalous Scientist

It was on a dark, quiet night in the science lab, nothing could be heard but the cackles of the evil scientist and the hissing of the boiling potions that he was creating to cause disastrous effects... The chemicals began to bubble violently, the stench from the smoke smelt like rotten eggs, the evil scientist began to panic. The poison had turned a fire-red colour, it began to burn through the lab. The scientist cried out, "Oh no what have I done?" The blood-red poison crept closer to the scientist, would he escape in time?

Lucy Phillips (12)
Maidenhill School, Stonehouse

Code 7

Bang! The bomb exploded. I couldn't stop it. My heart was pounding, it was all my fault. I couldn't breathe. The gases filled the room. I needed to crack the code to isolate the gas. But first I needed to get me and everyone else out of here. I found the emergency gas masks and protective clothing and raised the alarm. I gathered everyone up and led them out, thankfully everyone was safe for the moment. I really didn't know what the code could be, I needed to think. Wait, I've got it but will I be right?

Ruby Harris (12)
Maidenhill School, Stonehouse

In The Hole

I peered around the corner. There was a huge hole in the used-to-be busy road. You see, aliens have invaded Earth, bringing with them an awful disease. I could see the horrible, slimy creatures, pouring an odd fizzy green liquid into the hole. In the hole was the main water pipe for the entire world... I had to tell the survivors. Barely anyone was left on the planet. We had survived as our water pipe was broken; we mustn't mend it. I turned and cautiously crept away, back to base. I had saved the human race from extinction.

Imogen Threadingham (13)
Maidenhill School, Stonehouse

Can't Leave The Bunker

We finally emerged from the underground bunker, the disease had already spread. We knew we couldn't stay down here for long because of our small food supply. Every time someone with the disease touched someone else they would catch the disease. There was no way of escaping, we heard the trembling of them above us. It did not sound good, we were all going to die. We looked in all the books down here for a cure but there was nothing. We started this mess, we had to fix it before it was too late. Wait, what was that noise...?

Lara Lear (12)
Maidenhill School, Stonehouse

The Parasitic Fly

The rash is spreading, pulsing, hurting, it's burning my skin. The creature died but I turned into a parasitic fly, that is not cool. If someone else is this horrible creature, what has the creature done to me? My legs are turning into thin black legs. My arms are turning into wings and my eyes are going to be round black eyes and poison in my tail, maybe I can't control my body if I can kill myself before the time I turn into a parasitic fly. I have to kill the substance inside me so the disease doesn't spread.

Owen Jay Hudson (13)
Maidenhill School, Stonehouse

Darkness Awoke

I woke up cold from my dry bed. I lay there, opened my window and screamed. I saw darkness then... zombies just appeared out of nowhere. I got up and ran into the bathroom. I locked myself in. Ten minutes later I opened up the door then crawled straight back into my room, looked out of my window, they were still there crawling about hitting cars! I ran downstairs to find my mom on the kitchen floor. I screamed at her! She stood up from the floor but then something started to creak I walked over to the door... *Bang!*

Thalia Price (13)
Maidenhill School, Stonehouse

Will They Get Me?

The rash was spreading, pulsing, hurting. But where would we find a cure? The screams of people getting bitten were unbearable. But did we dare go up from underground? Would the animals get to us and was there anyone left up there? Then I lifted my head from underground, I saw the highly deadly fly coming for me. What would I do? Could I get to shelter in time? But as the words rushed through my head I felt faint and looked down at my arm. I realised I'd been bitten! "Please, someone, help me, take cover..."

Ellie Rice (12)
Maidenhill School, Stonehouse

Project Biohazard Department 20

My name is Dylan Ark, I'm a reporter. I had been working on the Genexia Cooperation report. I interviewed their boss, Winston Drake, about the tests and then I lost my job. But then I got a call from the employer of Genxiea and she said something was going on. She took me to the testing room. I took some pictures, I hacked into their computer, I saw something called the B Virus. They had an operation called Blizzard. I became infected; I ate and drank less - spaced out more. Then a day later the virus was released...

Kieran Reed Gowing (12)
Maidenhill School, Stonehouse

The Unsolved Mystery

The mysterious blinding box, we wondered what was inside. A blast of contamination seeped through the sides, one day I got too curious and had a look inside. I didn't know that zombies were alive? I trembled back the next day, the box was empty... I shivered and turned around to Death running at me! I ran up the dark alleyway but everywhere I turned, Death seemed to follow, just like a shadow. The roar of the half-dead beast, it was carrying the contaminated box. It wanted me inside. I felt empty, empty, empty...

Chloe Merrick (13)
Maidenhill School, Stonehouse

The Chosen One

Crawling. Itching. Scratching. What is it? Green. Why is my skin turning murky green? I look out into the distance and see the empty space that held healthy people. But they are no longer there. They lie unconscious on the floor that has now consumed them. Alive? I think not. My eyes are burning, my skin is on fire and I can't think about anything other than why...? Why am I the chosen one? What have I done? Wait... a man appears. I don't know it yet, but he has the answers to my questions. But I'm gone.

Zoe Barton (14)
Maidenhill School, Stonehouse

Gone! Forever!

I don't know how I got here, but all I know is that I am loving it here on Earth. I've been causing havoc everywhere, people are dropping off like flies and all you have to do is get in the water supply. The population is going downhill! The highest scientists have been looking for a cure but of course, I saved the day by infecting their solutions and chemicals. No one will be able to save the race now! It is the end, end of humanity. Next, I shall attack the animals until everything living is gone! Forever!

Georgina Knight (12)
Maidenhill School, Stonehouse

They Are Here...

Doctor Jhonny heard a knock at the door. A scratch then a sound. He knew what it was... He ran, ran as fast as he could. He picked up a chair then blocked the door and fled down the basement with his test tubes. The mutated creatures wanted the antidote. He had almost made it. He only needed to add a few more acids and toxins. To make the PH of the substance that when combined with the creatures the PH number is below neutral. *Smash!* They were almost here. The last drop fell into the test tube... Now what?

Ethan Robinson (12)
Maidenhill School, Stonehouse

Love Poison

The human race is all over me. Orla my crush. I gave her a stupid love potion but she had to have the flu. The whole world has gone love mad over me, just by one little cough. The love was spreading. In a way, I felt happy getting all the attention, but citizens of the world were killing each other. I found an underground bunker to hide in, it should keep me safe. *Bang! Bang!* "FBI open up!" The door flung open and the FBI took me into a cell, to bring peace to the world. Goodbye cruel universe.

Georgia Heaton (11)
Maidenhill School, Stonehouse

Would You Like Fries With That?

Breathing in and out, in and out with each step I took. Anxiously I approached the lab everyone was forbidden from. I opened the door and there was a man, his skin had turned a dark repulsive grey colour. There was only one answer, he had got the infection. A story came out in the news about an outburst of people dying. A woman had put poison in the deep fat fryer at McDonald's when people ate the food they would turn grey then die. So, here I was holding the needle, this man's life was now in my hands...

Maddie May East (12)
Maidenhill School, Stonehouse

The Time End

The unknown disease was spreading, it was made in a secure lab but it escaped. Fear, chaos, panic. Now few humans remain. It came from a genetically modified plant. We were too greedy, we wanted more. It now has a mind of its own and it is spreading as we speak, we have a slim chance of surviving this catastrophe. Resources are running low, we don't know what it is, why it is trying to kill us off. We have no idea how to cure it, but humanity's last survivors must fight, stop and cure the disease.

Edgar Alexander Ayers (13)
Maidenhill School, Stonehouse

The Infection

A horrific experiment has gone wrong and most of the world has paid the price. As this disease makes its way to the remaining survivors, a group of teenagers are trying to make it to the source of the disease and shut it down to save the human race from facing extinction. Few survivors take the trip to the source but now the problem is the disease power switch is at the top of the room. The survivors make a human ladder and make it to the switch and turn it off. They go to Buckingham Palace to live life.

Georgie Moss
Maidenhill School, Stonehouse

The Zombie Attack

"Doctor, I am a kid who saw a monster, but the monster started to eat people so it's not like your normal under-the-bed monster, this will change the world forever. Let's call the monster a zombie only because it looked like it was from the undead. When I saw the zombie it was eating a human, I didn't know what to do so I ran home to be safe but I wasn't safe, there was a zombie in my house eating my family! My dad was screaming telling me to run here, where I could find you..."

Kayla White (13)
Maidenhill School, Stonehouse

The Apocalypse

I knew that I had to run. Far, far away. It was too dangerous here, my heart pounded. This was it. The zombies were coming. Behind me were the other survivors. There was only four of us. As I looked behind me I saw one of the men fall down. The zombies were beside him in an instant. Trapping him. Infecting him. We couldn't help him, we had to help ourselves. The end was in sight. It was the factory or certain death. My stomach clenched in fear. Only a few more steps. That was all. Would I make it?

Elsie Hall (12)
Maidenhill School, Stonehouse

Project

The giant poisonous cloud rose into the sky and onto the people underneath it. It infected all of them except a few people that survived, they were protected from the cloud. The people that survived had to stay in a dome to stay safe from the people that had been infected. When we got in the dome we had no food to survive. I stood at the edge of the dome. I watched people bite and scratch other survivors that were outside of the dome. I felt scared for life. I will never go outside ever again. Ever.

Connor Ryan (12)
Maidenhill School, Stonehouse

Infected

Today was a dreadful day. I filled some plastic cups from the tap and decided to give it to the homeless and some other people as well. When I gave it to one of the homeless people they started to have a fit. All of a sudden, I realised the whole town was infected, I started to get surrounded by family and friends and even teachers. All of a sudden, I was woken by my mum, luckily it was a dream. I was relieved that my family and friends weren't zombies. I hope I never experience that in my life!

Noah Palmer (12)
Maidenhill School, Stonehouse

Zombie Round The Corner

I was looking far into the gloomy woods when I instantly heard a crack from a twig from behind me. I looked back but there was no one or nothing to be seen. I carried on walking and my knees were trembling and I was scared about what would be waiting for me around the corner. I was quickening up my pace now because I was too scared, then I turned around and saw a figure staring at me. Then it slowly started walking towards me and my knees started trembling. Then it got closer, it was a zombie...

Maddie Hobbs (14)

Maidenhill School, Stonehouse

The End Of The World!

I was walking along the road, what was that walking in front of me? A sea of weird-looking men walked towards me, then I realised - they were zombies. I studied them closer but why were they all men? I ran and ran and ran until... everything went black.

I woke up a tap on my shoulder. Wait, what? It was a normal man staring at me. I looked around and saw jars of a green substance. I asked the strange man what was happening and he simply replied with, "The end of the world."

Tyler Hinchliffe (12)
Maidenhill School, Stonehouse

The Scattering Shadow

A shadow scuttled by. I'd just seen a zombie movie so it was probably my mind playing tricks on me. I carried on walking and saw the same shadow scuttling past and to make it worse a street light was flickering. I was getting freaked out so I ran as fast as I could out of the road. I turned back around and there was nothing. But when I looked back round I saw a zombie staring down at me with his yellow eyes. I ran to the bridge, should I jump? Could I escape that horrible creature...

Theo Chandler
Maidenhill School, Stonehouse

A Touch Can Destroy Everything

A baby girl was born, but she had an unknown disease. After five years of living life she started to change and so did all of the people she had touched. Their skin burned. She started to touch everyone she passed. She had gone rogue but she kept waking up like she was just in a trance. Not many people were alive, but then out of the corner of my eye, I saw her. She came my way and she touched me. In a flash, everything was gone. I was a living skeleton wandering around the dead city.

Tamsin Meek (11)
Maidenhill School, Stonehouse

Chemicals

As the last drop fell into the test tube, Doctor Robert Jenkins knew he had doomed us all. The liquid bubbled onto the doctor's face and he said, "It is my time now!" He ripped the metal doors open and splashed the chemicals all over his colleagues. They were all infected. They scrambled to the streets and spilt the chemicals on everyone and everything. Survivors were limited, food was sparse. All they could do was sit and wait. What else could they do...?

Bailey Johnson (12)
Maidenhill School, Stonehouse

Mistakes

Hi, my name is Link or Pboo7. The human race is falling apart. A mad scientist tried making a cure for cancer but he put some rat poison in the mixture. The cure went around the world rapidly. So the humans went underground to live but the virus followed us. We lived in abandoned mines left in the 1950s. My dad is still out there with those creatures. It's up to me to stop the virus and bring people to safety but I will have to travel far to find them...

Taylor Pritchard (13)
Maidenhill School, Stonehouse

Contaminated

Zombies surrounded us from all angles, there was nowhere to escape from them. We were not safe anymore. We ran as fast as we could away from the zombies but they caught up with us and tried to bite us. Dad was lying on the floor in agony and I tried to save him but it was way too late. Zombies approached me but I managed to escape. I sprinted to the house but it was completely deserted. They were nowhere to be seen, maybe they got caught but nobody knows.

Callum Owen Greenaway (12)
Maidenhill School, Stonehouse

Leakage At Area 51

I was a scientist at Area 51 when it happened. The reactor core exploded out of nowhere and gas came leaking out. We all ran as fast as we could but my friend was still in the reactor room. I went back to see my friend just to find that my friend had become a mutant and he was running at me. I ran for my life and I dared to look back but then I tripped. My friend was standing over me then one of the guards shot my friend in the head and took me outside...

Ryan Brooks (13)
Maidenhill School, Stonehouse

Toxic Science Lab

We finally emerged from the underground bunker and we saw a toxic power plant with zombies leaking rapidly out of the shattered panes. There were only three of us left. The zombies had almost eliminated all of the entire human race. We needed to stop them and fast. We had not got enough food and water and only had one torch which was flickering. We had to find the healing potion soon or we would all die. Will we survive or not?

Melody Bragg (12)
Maidenhill School, Stonehouse

Mission Contamination

Most of the human race was wiped out by this horrible disease...

Three months ago... "Test Subject 4546B unaccounted for, code red, code red!"

A disease called Karra had infected the planet. Daniel Mcgavin and his friend Edgar Ware were the only survivors in New York. They had to survive with only a few shells in the shotgun.

"Come on, it's only a few miles to the rendezvous," said Daniel. "We are going to survive."

Slash!

"Arghh!" Edgar was infected. Now there were two of them and one shot in the shotgun...

Lewis Elliot Bryant (12)

Rednock School, Dursley

The Disastrous Matter

Dear Professor Macartney,
The infection has spread further. The amount of corpses pilled beside my disinfected house is indescribable. Screeches echo through the narrow streets of Parenmouth as beings are tortured by this unholy disease. I need help, you must come and save me before it's too late. Please, for the sake of mankind. You are the only one who knows. Currently, the disease has only spread to my toes but who knows how long it will take to unfold. Be quick but be careful not to contaminate yourself.
Yours sincerely,
Doctor Shallow
This is a do or die situation!

Kayti Miles
Rednock School, Dursley

Why Me?

I opened the soundproof, heavy, thick door with a struggle. Why me? The patches of white skin were becoming fewer by the day. Today, I'd been thrown into quarantine. All alone. Again I was asked a series of questions and given the blandest of food I'd ever eaten. I then started to hear a voice. It wasn't mine, it wasn't the officers...
Why don't you give up? You'll die soon enough, that was repeating in my mind for hours and for hours. I sat cradled in the corner of the room, screaming to myself.
"Could this parasite leave me alone?"

Eowyn Kathleen Barnes-Short (12)
Rednock School, Dursley

The Plague

"Hello, hello, is anyone there?"
That radio was our last fragment of hope and had
just shattered into a million unretrievable pieces.
We had been scavenging for days and trying to
survive on scraps of bread and our emergency
supplies had nearly run out. The world had driven
itself into the lair and couldn't get out.
For days now we have been recounting the last
few unforgettable glimpses of the plague. The
government had tried to insert particles of
titanium into humans to make them stronger. The
problem is it worked! The world is corrupted, no
place is safe!

Austyn Cole (12)
Rednock School, Dursley

Skin Crawling

Blood pulsed through my veins at an alarming rate and I felt something scuttle under my skin. Sweat trickled down my petrified face as I rummaged through a drawer in a desolate science lab, searching desperately for the minuscule flask that would put an end to this skin-crawling, blood-churning agony. My hand snapped as I whipped out the bottle and chugged the bitter-tasting contents down. Almost instantly the harrowing sensation of a creature crawling through my body ceased and I let out a deep exhale. I wiped the sweat off my face and smiled to myself. I saved myself.

Halima Wilkins (12)

Rednock School, Dursley

Mum? Are You Alright?

It was spreading. The violent airborne virus was killing millions. Their rotten vile corpses wandered around the street groaning, trying to find a human to feast on.

I locked the rusty garage door and grabbed the axe. Tears trickled like miniature rivers down the pale cheeks of my face. My mum groaned and hacked away at the door. She broke in...

I grabbed the axe and pulled it out of mum's rotting flesh. A bite mark stared at me. I stared at it.

The end was surprisingly close. I felt the virus spreading. I didn't want to be one.

William Johnson (12)
Rednock School, Dursley

The Deathtrap

I awoke, something was touching my grey skin. A series of thuds and screams came from outside my hospital room. I stumbled forward. "Aaarghhh!" There was a man. A dead man lying on the floor, eyes open, peering up at this cruel world. I covered my mouth as I heard someone coming towards me. Her hand stuck up, seeing her last ray of sunlight.

I was curious, I wanted to open the door. I did but I wish I hadn't. Corpses with rashes were lying around me. The scarlet rash spread up my body like a spider. Would I live?

Isabelle Fowler (12)
Rednock School, Dursley

Never Forget

April 4th, 2035. I had never seen this much death. It was like the Black Death all over again. I noticed my friend had quite a harsh rash. He advised me to never tell anyone about it. So I didn't. That was a mistake I will never forget.

One year later, nearly all of England's population has been wiped out. It is just me, Markus and James left. Everywhere is dull and desolate. I will never forget them, Mum, Dad, Alice, Ben everyone. If I live then I don't know what I'll do, but I will do something to help.

Thomas Lightfoot (12)
Rednock School, Dursley

The Day It Began

"The White House has released a statement issuing a worldwide quarantine. The following images could be disturbing for sensitive or young viewers... As you can see here Chelsea Football Stadium, London, several piles of corpses side by side.

This next image is taken from the forward view of our news helicopter in Cabot Circus, Bristol. A public quarantine. This is our final broadcast. It has been-"

He turned off the TV, reloaded his shotgun and waited by the door. This was the day it all began.

Billy Cadman (12)
Rednock School, Dursley

Infected

Boom! The science lab exploded and there was green ooze spilling out. I didn't know what was going in so I rushed outside and suddenly I felt nauseous. I wandered around a bit until I took a glimpse of a greeny, yellowy figure with a ripped lab jacket on. As they came towards me I noticed that they weren't a human at all, in fact, they looked like a zombie! I had to be dreaming! Zombies didn't exist. All of a sudden I felt dizzy. I fell to my knees. I knew it was the end of me...

Ruby Jean Chandler (11)
Rednock School, Dursley

Nowhere To Run, Nowhere To Hide

"They're coming!" the radio crackled. Who was coming? Our small group of survivors crept along the alleyway towards the city. We made it! We reached the large construction fence. I realised we finally had a shot at survival. As if we were in slow motion, we ran to the camp. Suddenly everyone stopped. Thousands of zombies crowded the streets. The camp had been invaded. We were done for. Our lives were over. Zombies closed in, blocking our exits. Nowhere to run, nowhere to hide!

Keeva Andersson–Gylden (12)

Rednock School, Dursley

The Secret

The heat warmed up my hands as I carried the tea to my mother. I walked into my mother's bedroom, she was sickly green. She told me if I ever got it, I was to keep it a secret and never show anyone. Soon my mother passed, so did my father.
The next morning I saw something, a green speck. The speck became a patch, the patch spread around my hand. I ran back to my house and hid under my crooked bed. Just then I saw a flickering. My time was up. I think.

Kitty Pain
Rednock School, Dursley

The Fall Of Civilisation

The rash was spreading across the country dangerously fast. People only had a few days to live. Luckily, I was safe for the moment but piles of bodies were strewn across the street outside ready to spread the infection. Most of the population had fled out of the country but they had only got sick. The president and other important people had been put in quarantine but the public had been blocked out. Left to die!

Miller Exell (11)
Rednock School, Dursley

Mission Contamination

Something scuttles under my skin. As the cogs in my brain begin to whir, the world before me refines from a pixelated block of colour to a crisp image. A mechanical voice slurs into my consciousness.

"Can you feel it?" it asks. "The scuttling under your skin?"

With those words, I know it's coursing through my veins, mixing with the oil and electricity that fuels me. The scuttling takes over my movements, controlling my arms, manipulating my software. I am at the mercy of the disease, for not a single robot has surpassed the virus's hold.

Error.

Error.

System malfunction.

Emiko L'Estrange (13)
The King's School, Ottery St Mary

Mission Contamination

The world's ending and it isn't my fault. How did I know that bunker 9 would be breached? The people were angry, tensions were mounting. We knew that, but we didn't know that it would go this far. As I begin to shrink, my last thought is, *it isn't my fault*. I tried to tell them. But they wouldn't listen. Nobody knew I was colourblind. Red was destroy, blue was release. Since we have got this far, I can only assume you know what happened. Now E27 is spreading through the world, and we can do nothing to stop it.

Daisy Copping (16)
The King's School, Ottery St Mary

Mission Contamination

"Noooo!" James screamed as the shelter doors closed with a slam, trapping him on the outside with the virus. He looked behind him and lost the ability to move. Slowly heading his way was a large green mist. Tears formed in his eyes as the mist engulfed him like a whale finally swallowing its prey. He felt his skin start to prickle and let out a blood-curdling scream as the virus attacked his body. He collapsed to the ground in agony as tiny organisms ripped him to shreds from the inside. Slowly, the boy known as James died.

Oliver Matthews (16)
The King's School, Ottery St Mary

Mission Catastrophe

I was a something once and now I am nothing. I used to make a difference, but people don't like difference. No one likes change. I changed the world and now I see myself as everyone else did. I'm the kid that just keeps going, even when they are told to stop. And now, I'm making humanity pay the price for my mistake. It is the last few months of humanity and everyone is trying to survive. But I know that no one will survive - because I made their killer and 'it' never misses! No one ever escapes... except me.

Scarlett Spencer

The King's School, Ottery St Mary

Carnage

"Mum?" No response. Something's wrong. The chills shiver through my body. In the distance I can hear a guttural screech. I don't know how to explain my feelings right now.

Down the corridor I can see a shadow careering towards me. The cacophonous screaming gets louder. Warily, I move in the opposite direction, heading for the bathroom. I find a myriad of body parts on my mum's bedroom floor. This creature has created absolute carnage. Terrified, I take a closer look, hoping not to see her silver bracelet. Trembling, I whip around as something vast lunges at me...

Daisy Earl
UTC Oxfordshire, Harwell

Their Blood Spills

"You hear it don't you?" he said as they stared into the flames.

"The growling, the hunger in their moans..." she sighed.

"Why?" a desperate cry rang out.

"Keep your voices down, they'll hear us," the first man warned.

"Why, you say? Because God wants to punish us, that's why," she said. "We went against his laws now hell is raining down upon us."

A bang ricocheted across the camp.

"Get ready. They are here..." Rifles cocked and fires were extinguished as the horde descended...

Sam Gillies
UTC Oxfordshire, Harwell

Hell's Incarnation

"Run, Jess!"

She woke in shock, sweat dripping from her forehead. It was the last human voice she'd hear. She knew she was the only one left. The world as she knew it had become overrun by creatures of the dark. Hell had crawled out of the ground.

Bang.

The door to the dilapidated, discarded WWII bunker flew off. Her biggest threat lumbered from the shadows; its eyes were obsidian black. It stood on its hind legs, its teeth protruding out of its snout, its body covered in thick scales. Its drool dripped like blood down a wall.

Run!

Sophie Bardell (15)

UTC Oxfordshire, Harwell

Abandoned

Coming back from the war in Iraq, I noticed the airfield was abandoned. Blown up choppers everywhere and rotting bodies. The bodies were surrounded by crippled, human-shaped figures, stumbling towards our chinook with evil intent in their dead eyes.

We landed and they charged towards us with hunger and anger. We prepared to leave. Until one lunged towards me, grabbing my arm and pulling me towards it. Then it bit a chunk off my neck leaving me prone on the ground. My neck started throbbing then everything started to go dark.

A burst of hunger and energy filled my veins...

Joshua Hughes
UTC Oxfordshire, Harwell

Outside

Weeks, months, years: who knows? It feels like years since it started but the memories are still fresh, although I wish they would rot into nothing. Living in the bunker was a strange feeling - no sense of time, direction or any knowledge of what's happening... probably nothing.
I can't remember the last time I experienced fun or joy. I don't even have any memories of joy left. The most fun we have is punching walls, which is not fun at all, but it's better than not feeling anything. Who knows what it's like outside anymore? I don't want to.

William Thorne
UTC Oxfordshire, Harwell

Aftermath

A lone robin flitters in a crisp, Tyrian-purple sky. Fading rays of sun illuminate a fragmented sprawl of shattered concrete and cracked steel beneath him. Over these antique ruins, rivulets flow, and canopies drown out the sight of the dilapidated streets he knows lurk underneath. In the distance, an iridescent smear coats a swath of ocean, stilling its dead waters. Faint hues of black and crimson line its edges. But the robin does not go there. Rather, it dives down to the crown of a nearby tree and roosts in wait for his mate. A shadow envelops the land...

Alex Morgan (14)
UTC Oxfordshire, Harwell

The Ash Dawn

The sun rose behind the ash cloud, illuminating the effects of the so-called Volcanic Winter.

As the cloud spewed up from Mount Yellowstone's mouth, consuming the blue sky, it took away the one thing we could rely on - air. The ash polluted it and betrayed us, transforming from our lifeline to our greatest threat. Inhaling would kill you in minutes. It exterminated more life than the bubonic plague.

My filtration mask itched my jaw as I stepped through the winter wasteland. I strained to see through the thick cloud. The sunrise was... dim.

Finnan James Bunce (15)
UTC Oxfordshire, Harwell

The Screen

The blizzard raged on. The TV was emitting a low buzz. There was three of us huddling around it. The dim glow was the only thing keeping our hopes alive, desperate for something to appear, to remember they were alive.

After a fearful hour, a face flickered onto the dim screen. His words cut through us like paper. "The world has fallen to an unknown disease. All people of the world stay indoors and do not interact with anyo-" He was dragged off by hands grasping from military sleeves. Screaming followed, then static took the screen.

Samuel Chandler (15)
UTC Oxfordshire, Harwell

Duty

Death. Contamination. War. It all started down in Los Almos National Laboratory. A wild tufted deer escaped the test enclosure with four others - they'd been exposed to a non-lethal variant of the poison Botulinum.

I currently happen to be serving as an ATF agent and have been called out of duty to fight against these now eight-foot-tall beasts. They can take a bullet through the heart and seem to be becoming more vicious after every man, child and woman they bite and infect with their nine-inch-long fangs. My time to protect is here...

George Ashby (15)
UTC Oxfordshire, Harwell

Vestiges

The door wasn't opening. I could feel it pushing against *something* on the other side. I used my shoulder to try to barge it open. It took me a few attempts but, eventually, there was enough room for me to squeeze through. I looked at what was blocking the door... A body. I gave it a light kick, but they didn't react. I pushed them so they were facing up, its face was gone. Nothing there but blood, bone and brains. A single crow flew down and started pecking at the vestiges of life.
I ran...

Aidan Shields (15)
UTC Oxfordshire, Harwell

The School Run Contamination

I stepped out of the front door and began my daily journey to school. I put my headphones in and watched as two joggers passed, one lumbering, the other sprinting - the first with a congealing liquid on them. I wondered what it was. When I got to school the gates were warped open. I thought a car crashed. In the locker room, three bullies were picking on their normal targets, a bit more viciously than before - one was sinking his teeth in the warm pink flesh of their target. I walked past reluctant to intervene.

William Cross
UTC Oxfordshire, Harwell

The Last Light

My gas mask filters are on their last legs. May as well just take it off, let the smog invade my body, whisk me away to someplace safe. But how can someone relax after being beaten and battered like this? My knife went dull long ago... My body is incapable of handling all this stress; the strain on my mind is making me see things that no person should ever see. Now I'm starting to question if these things are real. Maybe I'll just lie down for a while. Promise me you'll wake me up when I'm home?

Todd Joe Andrews (15)
UTC Oxfordshire, Harwell

The Aftereffect

We must stay in our zone, we cannot venture afar. It's an empty wasteland where death grows. The fruit on the trees is inedible, the water contaminated, and the air unhealthy. We may now have but a few supplies but we'll manage. Life may be hard, our spirits lowered and disease spreading, but when it looks like defeat and the dirt covers your feet, trying to keep us down, you must not give up. In the end, we will come out strong. It may be the end of what it once was but we can make this world anew.

Alex Johns
Woodeaton Manor School, Woodeaton

YOUNG WRITERS INFORMATION

We hope you have enjoyed reading this book – and that you will continue to in the coming years.

If you're a young writer who enjoys reading and creative writing, or the parent of an enthusiastic poet or story writer, do visit our website **www.youngwriters.co.uk**. Here you will find free competitions, workshops and games, as well as recommended reads, a poetry glossary and our blog.

If you would like to order further copies of this book, or any of our other titles, then please give us a call or order via your online account.

Young Writers
Remus House
Coltsfoot Drive
Peterborough
PE2 9BF
(01733) 890066
info@youngwriters.co.uk

Join in the conversation!

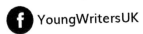 YoungWritersUK   @YoungWritersCW